THE BUBBLE-TASTIC ADVENTURE

P.G. WILLOW

Once upon a time, in a wild, colourful jungle, there lived three friends: Bubbles, the elephant, Gertie, the giraffe, and Charlie, the monkey.

Bubbles, the playful elephant, loved splashing in the nearby river, where cool, sparkling water danced around her trunk with each joyful splash.

Gertie, the tallest giraffe of them all, was never hungry. She could reach the sweetest, crunchiest leaves that no other giraffe could ever reach.

Charlie, a marvellously mischievous monkey, swung from bendy branches and made his friends giggle and squeal with delight with his silly tricks and funny faces...

Long ago, when Bubbles was a young calf,
she found a glowing bar of soap. Curious,
she took a bite and discovered her special talent...

"Ah...Ah...Ah...Ahhchooo!" Bubbles sneezed, blowing beautifully colourful bubbles from her trunk. From this day on, she became known as "Bubbles". When others called her this, she blushed and shyly lowered her trunk, feeling a bit different.

Ah...Ah...Ah... Ahhchooo!

One sunny day in the jungle, Gertie and Charlie were playing with a dandelion. They blew the fluffy seeds into the air. "Ah...Ah...Ah...Ahhchooo!" Bubbles sneezed, her colourful bubbles floated, glistening as they danced in the jungle breeze.

Charlie adventurously jumped onto a bubble and found that he could fly! Gertie's eyes widened in amazement. "Bubbles! These bubbles are magical!" Charlie exclaimed. "Let's use them for adventures!" They all agreed, excited to explore.

Bubbles thought carefully, tickled her nostrils, and blew three different bubbles: a small one for Charlie, a medium-sized one for herself, and a big, tall one for Gertie.

As a team, they glided above forests, peaks, and streams, the breeze ruffling their coats. They marvelled at the animals and breath-taking sights below, their hearts filled with wonder.

Touching down on a warm, sandy beach, Bubbles sent bubbles into the waves. As they burst, the water twinkled and sparkled like a dream.

The dolphins joined them, enchanted by
the magical bubbles. They dived and
splashed around, creating even more bubbles,
delighting in the magical playtime.

Bubbles inhaled deeply and blew a colossal bubble. The friends hopped on with glee, and the bubble carried them to a fragrant field of flowers.

Among the blossoms, they discovered a family of rabbits munching on carrots. Gertie, Bubbles, and Charlie exchanged excited glances, and they all hopped around playfully, giggling as they chased each other's tails.

"The laughter echoed as the bubble
lifted them back up,
whisking them beyond a radiant
rainbow and into a mystical starlit land.

There, they met Oscar, a wise old owl with warm, brown eyes. He softly whispered: "Young Bubbles, your bubbles are the key to fantastical adventures."

On their way home, Bubbles' eyes shone with joy, realising her uniqueness wasn't embarrassing but truly marvellous!

Gertie and Charlie hugged Bubbles tight,
grateful for the incredible adventure,
and beaming with pride for their fabulous friend.

Charlie chuckled, "I guess it's true what they say. Sometimes a little soap can go a long way!" The trio giggled with dreams of more bubble-tastic adventures.

Bubbles, Gertie, and Charlie all agreed to explore the world and make new friends together, all while blowing bubbles of all shapes and sizes.

Printed in Great Britain
by Amazon

28392813R00016